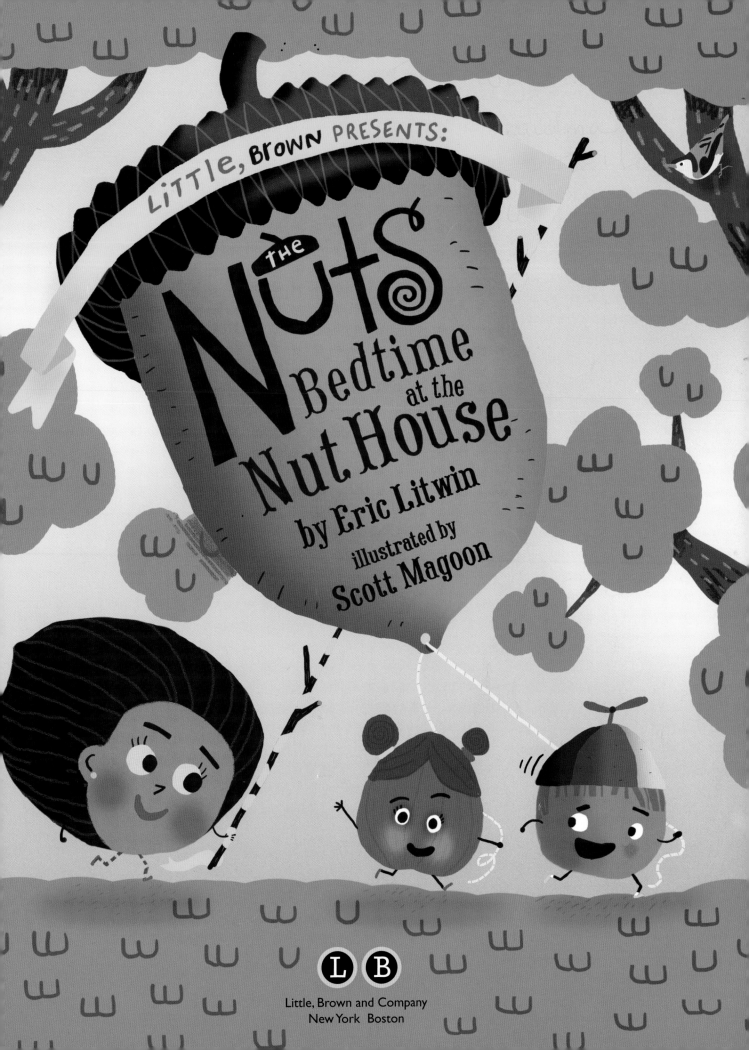

LITTLE, BROWN PRESENTS:

THE
Nuts
Bedtime
at the
Nut House

by Eric Litwin

illustrated by
Scott Magoon

LB

Little, Brown and Company
New York Boston

It was time for bed.
The day was done.

Nut House

Papa

But Hazel and Wally were still up having fun. And they sang together.

So Big Mama Nut
in her MAMA voice said,

♪ All little Nuts need
to go up to bed. ♫

Look, ↑
DIPPED
NUTS!

Sweet Hazel Nut would not go to her room.
She wiggled and giggled. She howled at the moon.

Then Hazel and Wally
kept singing their tune.

♪ We're Nuts!
We're Nuts!

We're
Nuts! ♫

So Big Mama Nut
in her **BIG**
voice said,

Wally Nut danced like a baby baboon.
He wiggled and giggled. He howled at the moon.

Then Hazel and Wally
kept singing their tune.

So Big Mama Nut in her **BIGGER** voice said,

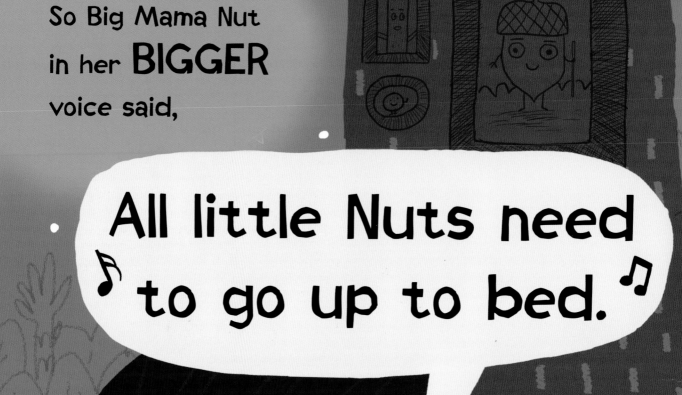

All little Nuts need ♪ to go up to bed. ♪

wally
2 months

Hazel
2 months

Wally
1 month

Hazel
1 month

Did Hazel stop singing?

No.

Did Wally stop playing?

No.

They had not heard a word
that their mama was saying.

They bounced up and down like two happy balloons.

Hee-hee! Hee-Hee!

They wiggled and giggled. They howled at the moon.

So Big Mama Nut
in her **BIGGEST** voice said,

♪ All little
Nuts need
to go up
to bed! ♫

ROASTED
CHESTNUT

Those Nuts did not budge.
Mama gave them THE LOOK.

She put her foot down. Her long finger shook.

She marched them to bed. She tucked them in tight.

Then just before Mama Nut turned off the light,
Hazel asked...

So Big Mama Nut said,
"No matter what,
you will always be
my sweet little Nuts."

And that nutty family
sang together!

And all was calm
and nutty
and right.

So Mama Nut turned off the light.
Good night, little Nuts, good night.

Extra Bonus
Nutty Lullaby

Good night, little Nut, good night.
Good night, little Nut, good night.
I love you the way you are.
You're my nutty shining star.
Good night, little Nut, good night.

Download the free song and lullaby, and have a nutty sing-along! TheNutFamily.com

To Arielle and Daniel. Two little nuts. —EL

For my family: Christy, Owen, and Daniel—I love going nuts with you! —SM

About This Book

This book was edited by Liza Baker and Connie Hsu, and art directed and designed by Patti Ann Harris. The production was supervised by Erika Schwartz, and the production editor was Christine Ma. The digital illustrations were created using Adobe Photoshop and a very nutty imagination. The text and display type were set in Skizzors, and the jacket was hand-lettered by the illustrator.

Text copyright © 2012 by Eric Litwin
Illustrations copyright © 2014 by Scott Magoon
Music produced by Michael Levine
Cover art © 2014 by Scott Magoon
Cover design by Patti Ann Harris
Cover © 2014 Hachette Book Group, Inc.

Little, Brown and Company

Hachette Book Group
237 Park Avenue, New York, NY 10017
Visit our website at lb-kids.com

Little, Brown and Company is a division of Hachette Book Group, Inc.
The Little, Brown name and logo are trademarks of Hachette Book Group, Inc.

The publisher is not responsible for websites (or their content) that are not owned by the publisher.

First Edition: July 2014

Library of Congress Cataloging-in-Publication Data

Litwin, Eric.
The Nuts: Bedtime at the Nut house / by Eric Litwin ; illustrated by Scott Magoon.—First edition.
pages cm
Summary: "Mama Nut says it's bedtime, but Hazel Nut and Wally Nut just aren't quite ready to stop the fun and go to bed"—Provided by publisher.
ISBN 978-0-316-32244-7 (hardcover)
[1. Stories in rhyme. 2. Bedtime—Fiction. 3. Play—Fiction. 4. Nuts—Fiction. 5. Family life—Fiction. 6. Humorous stories.] I. Magoon, Scott, illustrator. II. Title. III. Title: The Nut Family presents.
PZ8.3.L7387Bed 2014
[E]—dc23
                    2013041480

10 9 8 7 6 5 4 3 2 1

SC

Printed in China